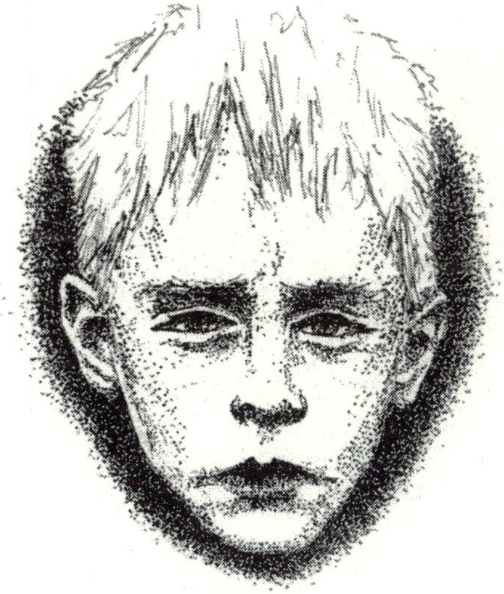

Published by Ad Hoc Fiction.
www.AdHocFiction.com

Purchasing Information:
Paperback available from www.AdHocFiction.com

E-book available from all usual outlets.
Printed in the United Kingdom.
First Printing 2021.

ISBN paperback 978-1-912095-29-2
ISBN e-Book 978-1-912095-28-5

Season of Bright Sorrow

by

David Swann

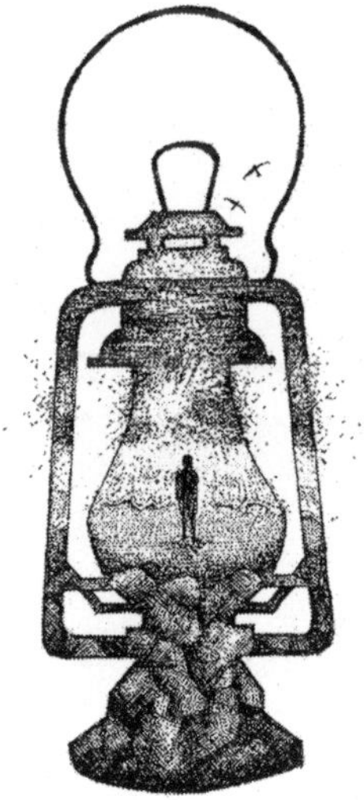

Illustrated by Sam Hubbard

AdHoc Fiction

‘**derelict (adj.)** 1640s, "left, abandoned by the owner or guardian," from Latin *derelictus* "solitary, deserted,"... "leave behind, forsake, abandon, give up,"... Originally especially of vessels abandoned at sea or stranded on shore. Of persona, "unfaithful, neglectful of responsibility," by 1864.’ -- Online Etymology Dictionary, derelict | Origin and meaning of derelict by *Online Etymology Dictionary* (etymonline.com)

Season of Bright Sorrow – a phrase sometimes used to describe the cold, sunny days of Lent, a time of both hunger and hope.

For the girls:

Ella Swann
and
Molly-Rose & Ivy-Star Hubbard

Contents

The line

When the hat came rolling across the beach towards Lana, it brought with it a memory of her dad.

Usually, these days, she struggled to picture her father's face, but now she recalled him watching Beyoncé on the telly, pretending his glasses had misted over, making as if the singer had blown his hat off. She remembered her mum bashing him on the arm, telling him to dream on.

It was sad if someone had lost their hat, but Lana wouldn't touch it, not now. She didn't like hats.

She climbed onto the rock that marked the end of her new territory, breathing salty smells, blinking in the dazzling light. She'd been raised in a narrow Pennine valley, so the bay's open spaces were thrilling.

Dangerous, too. Lana was careful not to stray from the path she'd agreed with her mother, an imaginary line between the sea and the boarding house. As long as she stayed on that line, her mother could see her from the window-seat.

Lana looked back over her shoulder, towards shore. Was that the distant shape of her mother, or light playing tricks on the glass? She waved, anyway. If you waved, someone might wave back, maybe a stranger on the promenade.

Set your clock

Here they came now, over the rim of the bay: the old man and his dog, one of them plodding solemnly into the salty wind, the other romping joyfully through the puddles.

A day couldn't start any better.

The old man, Mr Flook, had high standards. He knotted his neck-tie as tight as a whelk and kept his trilby at the correct angle, no matter how hard the wind charged in. As usual, he was putting items into the sack he always fetched with him: bits of plastic, shards of glass, the occasional brick or pipe…

Lana continued playing with the dog, a cross-border collie named Ringo, which spent its life chasing balls and licking faces.

'Is that daft article bothering thee?' asked the old man, evidently spotting Lana's frown.

Lana wiped mud off her jumper. Only her mum had touched her recently. The dog's paws had made her skin tingle. She shook her head. 'No,' she said. 'No, I like him.'

'Aye, well – you'd happen be less keen if you'd to worm him,' said the old man. His face was lined with as many channels as the bay. The channels narrowed when he bid her good day, and plodded away, limping under the weight of his beachcombing sack. She watched until the man and his dog were specks. There were quick-sands out there, and holes, and bracks, but the old man never waivered.

How pressed and stiff and clean he was, not a hair out of place. Yet the damage he was drawn to. Forever hunting for junk and roaming the derelict places.

You could depend on a person like that. You could set your clock by him.

In the bag

One straw hat.
Two mermaid's purses.
Needles.
Syringes.
Sea-glass (blue).
Two lengths of barbed wire.
Copper coin or token (unidentifiable).
Many plastic bottles, many bags.
Child's hair band.
Whelk shell (broken), plus egg-cases (attached).

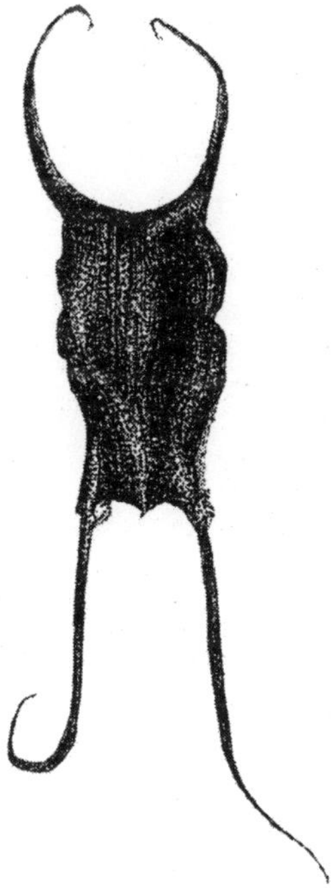

The Hole

There was a boy called Archie, about her age, maybe 12, who lived somewhere in the building. He sometimes stopped Lana on the landing, to pronounce a lot of guff. Today he claimed that the complete skeleton of a stagecoach rider had recently been found buried in a hole, out on the sands beyond the boarding house. The boy said that salt deposits had preserved the coachman. When fishermen stared into the hole, the rider looked exactly the same as when he'd been swallowed two centuries earlier. If a storm hadn't torn open the hole, the coachman might have lain there forever.

The boy had red eyes, as if he'd been staring into a bonfire. There was always a piece of white spit in the corner of his grey mouth. The spit quivered when he told his stories.

'That fella, he was still gripping his riding crop,' he said. 'It didn't matter how hard he whipped his horse, the tide here is faster.'

Lana edged around him. A boy like that, he was trouble on two legs. There was glee in his voice.

But she lingered on the stairs. 'The horse,' she said. 'What happened to the coachman's horse?'

Archie's face stared up through the stairwell, as pale as a root vegetable. His narrow eyes kept a gleam.

'They never found the horse,' he said.

The Living Waters

Her mother half-listened as Lana described her latest adventure on the bay. Meanwhile she went on watching the usual spot, somewhere beyond her daughter's left shoulder.

Lana turned, half-expecting to find someone standing behind her. No-one. Just the frayed brown room they'd been allocated by the social worker.

'He wanted me to give you this,' she said, placing a feather on the sticky vinyl table.

Shivering, her mother glanced at the feather. 'Who did?'

'Mr Flook, the beachcomber I told you about. To change our luck.'

'Honestly. Talking to strangers. How often have I warned you, Lana?'

Lana bit her lip. When they argued, no-one won. They just went round in circles. Better to study the line you walked every morning. Better to fill your head with the sea.

The boy was right: there were deadly places out on the bay. When it roared in, the tide galloped faster than any horse ever born. But the tides were bountiful, too. They brought the townsfolk food and fertilised their fields. Lana considered sharing these stories. She wanted to tell her mum the name given by the old man to the tides. The Living Waters, that's what he called them.

But her mother was watching the spot. Sometimes when Lara awoke at night from bad dreams and looked across the narrow room, she saw her mother's eyes glimmering, still watching the spot.

The Property

The landlord was sick of the place, too. '*Tell* me about it,' he said whenever Lana's mum went to complain about the geyser or radiators or taps.

But when she started telling him about it, he said: 'Exactly. I'm up to here with it all, too…' And then he listed his grievances against what he called The Property. Its plasterwork was mouldering, its masonry bulging. Tiles had buckled in the bathrooms. Toadstools were flourishing in places they'd no right to.

'*Toadstools*?' said Lana's mum.

'In the keyholes, and that.' He wiped his cadaverous face. The plan had been a B&B. But then the tourists stopped coming and his wife fell ill. So he was stuck with it, the family curse. At least his tenants got their views. He was stuck in the basement with an ailing wife.

The new plan was demolition, sell the land to Lidl. Meanwhile he'd squeeze what he could from the council, take whatever desperate characters they pushed his way.

He prided himself on being frank with his tenants. If the windows stuck and condensation ran down the walls, there was very little he could do. He was a victim of The Property too. 'I barely make it upstairs these days, my chest's that bad. Black rot, I call it...'

Lana watched him cough. He was sick like his house. The walls in the front passage had worn so thin, the wires of a disused phone system were poking through. Lana always rushed past, doing her best not to linger. But sometimes she couldn't help it, she looked. It was the sight of the wires, laid bare like that, all scraped and raw. They were like parts of a body that didn't work properly anymore. Like nerves.

Closed

After it rained, when it was dark, Lana liked to walk past the amusement arcades, where the puddles swam with glossy colours that made her shoes mysterious.

The arcades themselves were dismal, their carpets frazzled, their neon lights flashing for a handful of regulars.

Lana passed a row of derelict shops. The metal shutters had been scribbled over with impenetrable sigils: DOBBO, KINCAID, YOGURT.

Looming beyond was the loop of a derelict big dipper, slowly disintegrating in the rain. The fun-fair's entrance was a giant plastic mouth, said once to have swallowed thousands of tourists. Now the mouth had lost all but four of its fangs, and was closed off by a gate marked with a sign: 'CLOSED DUE TO CIRCUMSTANCES'.

When Lana leaned on a metal shutter to get a better look at the mouth's decaying teeth, the shutter moved like a living thing. Further down the prom, when she looked back, the shutter was still trembling.

Soul

The bay, though. As soon as you got the door open, it punched you in the face. All that space and air. The sands fizzing under your windows. You forgot you were a Desperate Character. The wind blew over the flats and took your memories with it. Then you were like a spat or a lugworm, some tiny thing that lived in the sand. You didn't need a mind or a soul. The sand was your mind, the bay your soul. You didn't need to think about the friends you'd left behind or the place your dad had gone. You dug a hole and hid in it, and that was enough.

School

When Lana woke with a violent start, her teacher was standing above the desk.

'*Tired*?' she asked, more disappointed than angry.

Lana sat up straight, afraid she'd been swallowed by a hole. 'No, miss,' she said.

'Then I'd better raise my game and try to be more interesting, eh?'

Lana blinked. Under the strip-lights, her eyeballs felt raw. The lights turned everyone's skin into corned beef. The kids on the row behind were sniggering. La-la Lana, they called her. Lana the Backward Banana.

The other classes were taught by people who looked like they'd been made in sheds, but Miss Rogers smelled of apples. When you talked to her, she listened with the whole of her face. Sometimes she repeated the words, as if she needed to learn them for a test.

Lana had lost the fight to stay awake while Miss Rogers was talking about anxiety, the disease of their age. Anxiety made everyone small and unimportant, the teacher had been saying as Lana drifted away.

The opposite of anxiety was wonder, Miss Rogers said. Lana had laid her face on the desk, enjoying its coolness against her cheek. In a state of wonder, your smallness felt like a miracle, not a curse. You were a tiny part of everything that lived. You weren't separate from everything, you were joined to it.

'Take stars,' Miss Rogers had said. 'That's where carbon's made. That's where *you* were made.'

Hard to describe how it felt, to fall under the teacher's spell.

While Miss Rogers was talking, Lana forgot the mug-tree on the sink and the toadstools in the key-holes. She forgot the smells on her mum's breath and the curses she muttered in her sleep. It didn't matter that she'd left all her friends far behind in another town, or that the kids in her new class called her names. While Miss Rogers was talking, even the scratches in the desk felt nice against Lana's face. Even the foul words boys had gouged with broken biros.

She looked up at Miss Rogers, unable to explain.

Her teacher passed on, shaking her head.

On the row behind, they went on whispering. Whatever it was they were saying, Lana tuned it out. She'd got good at that recently. Sometimes she tuned herself out, too.

Spider

Lana wondered where her thoughts were. Inside her head? That didn't feel right. She imagined the thoughts hovering just above her, written into a comic-strip bubble.

If her thoughts could be written in words. As soon as she started to think about her thoughts, it became hard to tell *what* they were, let alone where.

She was on safari again. That's what Lana and her mum had taken to calling their showers. This was because of the wildlife that lived in their landlord's bathroom: mould on the tiles, lichen in the wainscotting. Also, mosquitos that hadn't been told it was winter in northern England, and they ought to be dead.

Best of all: the spider.

It was the spider that had made Lana wonder where her thoughts were. She'd been studying the spider for days, watching it weave its web. Did the spider change its mind whenever it met obstacles in their landlord's horrible bathroom? When it couldn't put the web where it planned because of a new bulge in the wall or an encrusted pipe?

Did a spider *have* a mind? If so, where? Inside the spider's head? Its thorax? Its disgusting legs?

Or did part of the spider's mind live inside its web?

Maybe a spider's mind stretched further than a person's. Maybe that silly little spider, living its obscure life in the furthermost crevice of a soon-to-be-demolished building, was freer, and made more decisions every day, than Lana did.

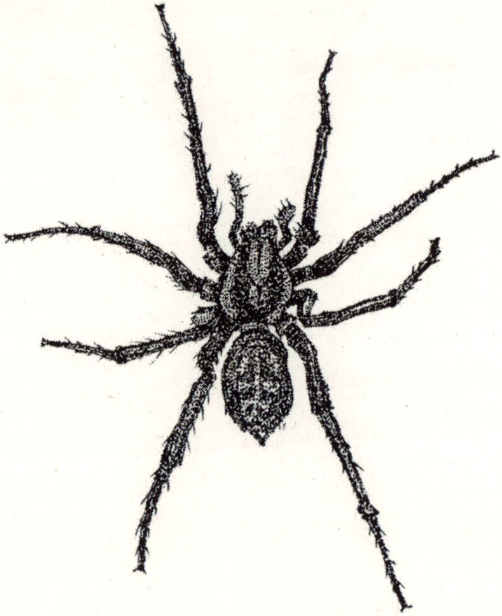

Obvious porridge

'It's not like one of them corny old Tarzan films they show on Sunday afternoons,' said the boy. He stayed where he was, blocking the door, stopping Lana from getting in. 'According to them daft old flicks, you sink up to your neck in porridge. In obvious porridge.'

Lana waited. She'd perish on the doorstep unless she asked him what it was really like to die in quicksand.

He wiped his eye. There was always something it, always a bit of ash or grit.

'What's it *really* like, then?' she said, finally.

'To die in quicksand?'

Lana looked at her watch.

'I'll tell you what it's really like,' Archie said. 'It doesn't suck you down – it sets around your shins like cement. Then you'd better hope somebody hears you screaming.' He pointed into the bay. 'Because if nobody hears you screaming, they'll dig you out the next day, and the last thing you'll have seen was the tide coming in towards you.'

He seemed satisfied with this information. 'Imagine that,' he said.

She did. That was half of Lana's problem. She was obedient. She did everything she was told.

The Skear

Normally her mum would open the boarding house window to shout a warning if she passed the skear. But today there was no shape at the window, so Lana kept going, towards the river.

Tides. Paedophiles. Quicksands. Her mother had itemised the dangers while Lana listened, resisting the urge to object. She'd experienced enough rows to know how useless they were. Rather than arguing, she waited till her mum passed out again, then slipped away.

With no-one watching, she decided to go to the river. It was further than she'd previously dared to venture. The river's water was black, its banks grey. There was something perfect about the mournful channel, how smooth it was, how it kept all the light it swallowed. Her boots squelched as she approached. At high tide, you couldn't see the river, but it was always there, at the foot of the sea. Whatever the time or the tide, it never stopped.

She watched a twig slowly curl away on the stream. The twig went where it was taken. Lana and her mother were twigs, too.

On shore, the row of boarding houses was like a streak of jam, spread thin over a sandwich. Her tummy rumbled. She'd probably go back, cobble together some lunch from whatever remained in the fridge.

Yet she dallied, studying corrugated lines left by the sea. Close to the skear, the water had run at cross-angles as it sloshed around the rock.

When she climbed onto the rock to inspect the lines, a shiver passed over Lana's skin. Two puddles had formed like eyes above a channel as sharp as a nose. There was a frond of sea-weed at the base of the chin, and pinched lines around the mouth.

She saw it straightaway: the goatee-beard, the scar.

The sea had drawn her dad's face.

It was almost a relief when she saw the distant figure of her mum banging on the window, demanding to know what the hell she was doing.

In the bag

Generous length of fencing twine.
Copper coin or token (unidentifiable).
Needles.
Syringes.
Many plastic bags, many bottles.
One red brick, stamped: ACCRINGTON.
Sea-glass (green).
Half of one starfish.
A child's glove (black), the elastic still attached, but its twin missing.

Reasons

Needles. Syringes. Plastic stuff, too. Lana understood the pollution's dangers. But why collect stuff that posed no threat? It must have been back-breaking, always carting that massive sack over the beach. Solemnly, the old man agreed with a shake of the head: he was wrong in the box, he surely must be. It was difficult to explain, but he had his reasons, as folk always do – not that their reasons always make sense, he knew that all too well, having lived as long as he had. 'Even at your tender young age, you'll have met a few rogues, lass – folk who act like butter wouldn't melt in their mouths… yet the wrongs they've done because of their reasons, and that innocent look in their eyes, as if you'd have done exactly the same wicked thing if you'd been wearing their shoes!'

Shielding her eyes from the sun, Lana tried not to blink; she'd seen an actor on telly talking about blinking, saying that the eyes were the seat of a person's power, and also of their vulnerability – that the twitch of an eyelid could condemn an enemy to death or undermine a nation's faith in their leader. It was hard to stare like that, though – hard not to blink as she watched the old man readjust his tie's knot to the periwinkle setting, then shift his sack to the other shoulder. He was embarrassed, Lana could tell – he'd spotted the look on her face after he criticised wicked people and their reasons. Well, then, that made two of them – because Lana had hurt him, too. He'd blinked when she asked about the sack. And she'd sensed his burden. Sensed two weights. Absence. Yearning.

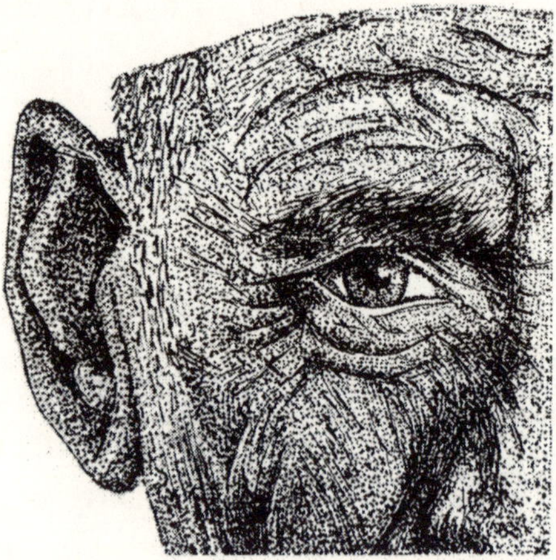

Ordeals

If she wasn't comatose or guarding the window, Lana's mum was usually in bed, watching TV when she returned from school. Her favourite programmes were about survival ordeals.

'You'd never even see a mountain lion. It'd creep up on you,' she said, glued to the screen. 'Like that postman there, in Vancouver. He was cycling, and it ripped his neck out.'

'Charming,' replied Lana, throwing down her satchel.

'In the *suburbs*,' said her mum, frowning at the screen.

Lana peered into the fridge. She'd have to start hunting soon, the way things were looking in there.

'This woman they're showing now, she climbed a tree. They told her: if a bear attacks, climb a tree. But the bear climbed up, too.' Her mum listed earlier ordeals: a polar bear that circled a shack for a week. A cougar that followed a hiker down a remote canyon. 'He did what they said: walked backwards steadily. But it just kept coming,' she said.

It would have been good to hear the awe in her voice, if she hadn't chosen to waste it on a documentary full of clanging noises. Most of the interviewees looked like they deserved to be eaten. There was an Outback hunter who stumbled upon a man-eating crocodile in a billabong. Also, a golfer who met a wolf.

'When he was about to make a putt,' said her mum.

'Good,' said Lana. 'I hate golf. They should all be eaten when they do putts. Turn it off, Mum. Let's get some air.'

Her mum shuddered and went on scratching the eczema on her hand. 'You discover things,' she said. 'Things you'd never have known. The right behaviour, in an ordeal.'

'In a remote canyon,' said Lana.

Her mum nodded.

'What the hell's a billabong, anyway?' Lana asked.

'Shhhh,' said her mum. 'Shhhh, they're showing the mountain lion again.'

The mouth of Karen Carpenter

On bad mornings, when the hangovers were proper stinkers, Lana put the toast straight into her mother's mouth, and muttered little encouragements.

Then she went round the flat, finding pills in various nooks & crannies – the back of the settee, a drawer in the table. It was good to flush it all down the toilet, even though she guessed there was probably plenty of other stuff stashed away in cunning places.

Afterwards she lay on the bed, stroking her mother's hair. 'As good as new,' she promised. 'Soon everything will be as good as new, Mum.'

Somewhere deep down inside the drugged-out trance, her mother was purring like a cat, a sound so perfect and natural it could have come from the mouth of Karen Carpenter.

When she heard her purring like that, Lana believed the silly promise she'd made. As she stroked her mum's hair, she believed that one day soon there would be a knock at the door and her mum would walk in a straight line to answer it. And she'd find her husband waiting on the step, apologising for all the fuss and bother, but could he come in. Could he come in and explain.

Then Lana's mum would believe the promise, too. And she'd say: Yes, certainly. Come in, you silly man. Come in and explain.

Laughterhouse

Their landlord had a shifty-looking stoop. You heard him gasping on the landings. There was nothing on him, only skin and bone. He was fixated on the power-points. He shuffled round the building, patting the walls. Afterwards he wiped his hands down his slacks.

Lana's mum couldn't bide him. On the rare occasions she planned to go out, she waited at the window until she was sure he'd left. Otherwise, she'd find him, lingering like mildew in a crevice.

Then she'd get The Full List:

Aye, the wife was badly again. Angina.

Their dog, too. Rex. Going off its back legs, the poor thing.

Not to mention: mange. Big fistfuls of hair. Plus, the tapeworm they got out of it. Unspeakable, that thing. It…

Myself? Well, soldiering on, thanks for asking. Of course, I'm a martyr to my bunions. The swellings have…

The tapeworm and the bunions, those were enough for Lana's mum. She squeezed her daughter's hand and pushed her through the old hotel, making up some lie about errands.

'What's a tapeworm, Mum?'

Lana's mum shushed her. Normally a street would be enough to give her the horrors. But now she had to get out, she had to get out.

In the street, round the corner, she leaned against a wall. At first, Lana thought her mother was having another attack. You got attacks after losing your confidence.

But she was laughing. Laughing more than Lana had ever known. Laughing like an asthma-patient. 'Bloody hell,' she said, recovering, wiping her mouth. 'Christ almighty.'

'OK, Mum?'

'Look,' she said, parting her lips. 'These are what they call teeth, lass. Folk used to see them. When I talked and laughed.'

Lana had no idea what she was talking about. She was acting like she did when she got on the sleep-medicine. Saying mad stuff. She went on down the prom ahead of her mother, thinking of the noises out of The Property's telly room. Some bloke from Carlisle went in there with boil-in-the-tin steak pies that he ate off his knees in the dark. He barked at every joke in every comedy, never altering his laugh. So that's what you heard all evening, through the floorboards: the laughs of an unhappy man who found everything a joke.

Good and gone

His cakehole, true. His cakehole, he struggled to tame. Plus, certain memories surged through the siege-lines.

Everything else, though: eyes, nose, ears, fingers. Archie had a tight rein on all that tackle. Every day he bunked off school and trotted over the sands, alert to the trembling quicksands, the mournful songs of the curlews. He was training himself like a device. If a redshank landed on a fence-post, the needle quivered inside him.

There were two worlds: the town and the bay. The town gave you Asdas and nail clinics, gave you vaping-gear and betting-slips. As for the bay, Archie didn't know what it offered. He'd no idea why he looked for the ribs of stranded boats or listened carefully to the gurglings of creeks. It wasn't nice out there, usually it was horrible. Wind stung your eyes, mud bubbled through your shoes. You were always blowing on your hands, having to double back, go the other way. What looked like solid ground turned out to be a bog. When you were certain you'd found a path, you sank up to your knees in a river.

Shivering now, his toes gloopy with mud, Archie peered towards shore, almost wishing he was there, almost wishing he was warm. He studied the nuclear power station, visible from all points. It looked as if someone had dumped a massive car battery on the beach. There was a sun under the roof of that building. The people there, they lived on the same street as a god.

There were two worlds: one that was visible and one nobody had ever seen. One of the worlds contained newsagents and fishmongers. The other existed only in glancing thoughts and shivers.

Archie forced down the memory that was trying to squeeze through. He'd keep his cakehole shut today, not think about his dad, not make the usual boasts and threats.

He'd stare at boats and listen to creeks, until he was good and gone, and the bay's emptiness filled him.

Spy-glass

Sometimes the old man let Lana peek through his telescope, which he carried everywhere like a pirate. She was always dizzy after squashing the bay into her eye. Curlews loomed up like pterodactyls. The stumps of distant jetties became skyscrapers.

He liked to keep an eye on the state of play, that's how Mr Flook described his vigils. To casual viewers, the bay was a boring place where nothing ever happened.

Until it did. Until a storm, say. In storms, rivers had been known to shift to new channels. If that happened, you may as well rip up your map. The wrecks out there on the sand, they told the stories.

He took the telescope back from her and did a slow 360-degree turn, keeping it fixed to his wrinkly eye. 'That way too,' he said. 'On land as well as sea. Wrecks wherever you look, and another old wreck doing the looking.'

Cemetery with lights

Locals snuck down back alleys to escape them! Aye, back then, tourists poured thick as gravy off the trains from Yorkshire. That thick, there were loudspeakers blaring out hotel vacancies.

Dolphins, too. I remember those characters at the outdoor swimming stadium. What a gleam they carried, enough to brighten any day!

Aye, the stadium's gone, as well. Gone the same way the dolphins went.

Like the piers: one to a storm, the other to a fire. No trace at all, except maybe a few coins in the sand, from when the slot-machines toppled overboard. Get down on the beach with your shovel, lass. You might find treasure.

You're fifty years late for the real treasure, though. We had two of everything, once. Not only two piers. Two towers. Two fairgrounds...

Listen at me. I was one of the daft buggers that snuck down the alleys, so I'm happen not as fussed as I make out. Still. Eight picture-houses, five theatres. Makes you think, eh? George Formby. Gracie Fields. Larry Grayson. Aye, all the big names. You'd have the time of your life, if you liked laughing.

If you didn't? Well, those that didn't like laughing, they went to Fleetwood.

One of the theatres was so big, it made you dizzy. I know because I met my wife in it. Picked her face out from three thousand! Fourteen dressing rooms, it had. Think about that the next time you walk through the car park. Laurence Olivier got changed there once, in one of those white boxes.

A cemetery with lights, that's what comedians call the place now.

You could do worse, I suppose. They can't demolish the sands or pull the shutters on the sunsets. And it isn't Burnley. They ought to put that on the brochures, eh? *Better than Burnley*. Bring them flocking, that would.

Another heyday? A rebirth? Aye, it's a nice idea, lass. But there aren't usually second chances, not when a town loses its purpose. You keep that lamp burning, though. The problem with old buggers like me, we fall asleep all the time, yet we've stopped dreaming.

And it's dreams we need now, love. Without dreams, there'd be nowt to wake up for.

Jolly Roger

Whatever had happened that day, it must have been bad. For the first time in weeks, Lana's mum had left the flat, alone.

It was amazing to see. Walking home from school, Lana found her mum on the promenade, waving what turned out to be a beer towel. It had a pub's name on it: The Star & Garter.

Also, she was singing The Jolly Roger.

The flag moved to half-mast as she made out her daughter. 'Lana,' she said, swaying. 'There you are, sweetheart.'

She gave that heart-breaking smile she'd been known for, a smile of pure surprise. 'I went out for… for a few things…' she said.

'Yes,' said Lana, taking the beer towel and linking arms.

'But they'd run out of most of… most of the stuff I was… I was after…'

Lana guided her in a straight line. 'Let's get you home and into bed, Mum.'

'I'm not drunk, love.'

'I know you're not, Mum.'

'I just need a nice warm shower, then a bit of telly to settle me down, love. Something quiet, happen with a few sheepdogs in it.'

They struggled down the prom, and for once Lana didn't study the mudflats, looking for those mysterious paths the boy claimed to follow. Instead, she concentrated on the nice scent her mother somehow gave off, even after a long drinking session.

There weren't any builders anywhere because the resort was falling down, but if there had been, one of them would have wolf-whistled. Builders always did when they spotted Lana's mum.

They'd driven her dad to the far end, the builders. He'd blamed his wife for encouraging them.

But when she changed her outfit, he said she'd let herself go.

Agoraphobic

Not full-blown, not like some of them. Not a mental patient.
Not the way they describe it in the magazines. Not a fear of open spaces. Not a fear of fields.
Not making it clear, she knew. Not an easy thing to talk about, though.
Not as bad when she left the house in company, no. Not when she left with her daughter.
Not to say the fear was gone. Not to say it was never not there.
Not only while it was happening, also while she was waiting for it to happen.
Not the monster. Not the space beneath the bed. Not those two things, but the number you reached when you added them together, the third thing that no living person had ever seen or touched.
Not that she really knew she meant.
Not that she was calling herself a monster. Not exactly, no.
Not when there were so many other things to worry about.
Not with all the chores that needed doing, the cooking & doing, the Hoovering and what not.

The other side

The boy wanted to know why she was always sitting on the rock.

'I sit on it at low tide,' she said. 'The rest of the time, it's underwater.'

'So?'

'So I *don't* sit on it all the time.'

'But when you do sit on it. What are you looking at?'

'The other side,' she said, pointing across the bay.

'What's so good about the other side?'

'It isn't this side,' she said.

'It would be if you were over there.'

Lana thought about that. The boy was less stupid than he looked. But he looked like a parsnip, so that wasn't difficult. 'What are *you* always doing out here, anyway?'

Archie smiled, secretly. His shoes were scumbered with mud. His freckles were hard to distinguish from specks of filth. 'I'm not always out here,' he said. 'I'm only here…'

'… at low tide,' they said, together.

She did the sarcastic applause she'd learned from her dad. '*Really*, though. *Really*, what are you looking for?'

'Paths,' said the boy. 'I'm looking for paths no-one else can see.'

A cold wind was blowing between them. Lana held the hair off her face. 'Why are you looking for paths?'

'For when I need them,' said the boy. 'In case I have to vanish.' He stooped to the sand and scraped off a few flakes of sand. Then he laid his palm flat and blew the flakes off his hand. 'Like this,' he said. 'Whoosh.'

The boy looked at her for a long moment, as if to say: I bet that impressed you, eh?

It did, but that wasn't the point.

'Anyway, I wish I'd time for prittle-prattle,' said the boy, in a faint Scottish burr. 'But I'm extremely busy. I've a lot on.'

Lana watched him stalk away. Like a fox, he looked back over his shoulder a few times. A sly one, for sure – the sort of kid who'd find a hiding place even out there, in the massive blank of the bay.

'If I don't see you through the week, I'll see you through the window,' he called back.

Lana did the fake laugh she normally saved for distant uncles. 'Not if I see you first,' she whispered.

The No Show

No, said her mum. No, she failed to see how regular contact with a monster could possibly help her daughter's development.

After everything he'd done? After what he'd put them all through?

No, she wouldn't re-consider her decision. Or consult the girl for her thoughts on the matter.

What was he waiting for, the short answer or the long one?

Yes, the long answer would be different from the short one.

The short answer: NO.

The long answer: N-O-O-O-O-O-O-O-O-O-O-O-O-O-O-O-O.

Did she have to howl at the moon?

Or maybe she should spell it out for him?

En. Oh.

No.

Now which of those two letters could he not understand?

Yes, said another voice. The voice of the case worker. Yes, he understood she'd changed her mind. But they'd made an agreement, hadn't they? To move here, for the sake of the girl?

Yes, there were difficult issues to work through, he agreed. After everything her husband had done. After what he'd put them all through.

No, the case-worker didn't regard himself as having the feelings of a stone.

Yes, but monster was a big word.

Not literally, no. But the same goes for yes. Yes is a short word, too.

No, he wasn't bullying her to say yes.
Yes, if it was happening to him, he'd howl, too.
Yes, he'd done a fair bit of basic spelling at school.
He wasn't proud of his sarcasm, no.
Yes, but we all have our limits.

The beaker people

The look on their faces when they caught Lana listening at the door, you'd have thought it was a crime to eavesdrop.

If it was a crime to eavesdrop, then those circles on the wall were a crime, too.

'Skulking about the place!' said her mother.

'Nearly brained you with the door!' said the case worker.

Lana laid her satchel over the back of the chair and went and stood by the circles, where the case-worker might see them, if he had actual eyes. The circles had been printed into the wallpaper by the beakers her mum used as listening devices. She pressed so hard when she was eavesdropping, the walls of their flat looked like Venn diagrams.

Someone on the other side of that wall was cracking up.

Someone on the other side of that wall blundered around, knocking things over.

And weeping. Someone on the other side of that wall was often found by the beakers to be weeping.

'What do you have to say for yourself, lass?'

'Nothing,' said Lana. She meant it. If she said nothing, there'd be no words to fill any beakers. If anyone was listening on the other side of the wall, Lana would break the chain.

That was a phrase her mum had used earlier against the case worker.

Breaking the chain? Alright, if that's how you want to phrase it. Yes, I'm breaking the chain. But it's better to break chains than allow that bastard to break my daughter's heart again. Have you got that? Are you writing that down in your pad?

Yes, said the case worker. Yes, I'm writing that down in my pad, Mrs Deacon. The literature, though. I'd like to leave you some literature.

I'll put it straight in the bin, she promised him.

That's your prerogative, Mrs Deacon. All I can do is offer you the options.

The options, said Lana's mum. I'm sick to death of the options.

Open Visit

No jewellery or hair-bands. Skirts must reach within two inches of the knee. No slits. No camouflage. No boob-tubes. No spandex or leggings.

Arrive early, for security. Have your Visiting Order ready. You will be asked to open your mouth. Guards will pat you down, or search you in other ways. A photograph will be taken, and documentation checked. Any irregularities, you will be sent away.

No food, except the food you buy in prison.

Expect dogs.

If dogs are in operation, do not pet the dogs.

Brief embraces are permitted at the start and end of visits. Occupy allocated seating. Hand-holding is usually forbidden. Kissing is not allowed.

Expect a big room, and noise. Guards may listen in. Your inter-actions will be videoed. Nothing should be passed to the prisoner.

Visits can be cut short without warning. The penalty for trafficking illegal items is arrest, followed by a visits ban, and/or closed visits. In closed visits, the prisoner may be separated from family members by a screen.

If you are under pressure to carry in drugs, speak to staff at the visitors' centre.

N.B. Some jails do not have visitors' centres.

Entanglements

Archie, the boy from upstairs, was keen that Lana should know his dad was a frogman. 'He lives on an oil-rig,' he said. 'That's why you won't see him much, apart from next week when he flies home in the oil company's helicopter. Unless there's another entanglement, of course.'

Lana had absolutely no idea what the boy was talking about.

'Sometimes he has to swim down to the sea-bed, to solve problems.'

'Problems?'

'If there's a leak in the pipeline, or a massive cable gets tangled. In a better world, my dad would be more famous than Tom Hanks. I mean, what's Tom Hanks ever done?'

'Acted in films,' said Lana.

'Exactly. But he's never untangled a cable, I bet.'

Lana shrugged. She wanted to get past, but the boy had taken root on the landing, grown into the carpet like a prickly weed.

'What's *your* dad do, then?' Archie asked. It sounded more like a taunt than a question.

'He's in prison,' said Lana. 'He had a fight in the pub, and he killed a man.'

Archie stepped back, into the stairwell's shadow. 'As if,' he said, rubbing his chin.

There was a gap now, and Lana darted through it, down the stairs.

Behind her, Archie seemed to have recovered from his shock. '*Killed a man*!' he shouted. 'Drives a bus, more like!'

She wanted to tell the boy to invent as many stories as he liked. It was obvious he was good at lying. But the strange thing was, he'd been right. Lana's dad *had* driven a bus, once, before what he now called the incident.

She kept going after she'd slammed the front door. She ran until she was far out over the sand. Then she looked down into the glitter left behind by the tide, and found a puddle with her face in it, and she stamped hard, until the scoop in the ground was dry and her face was only mud again.

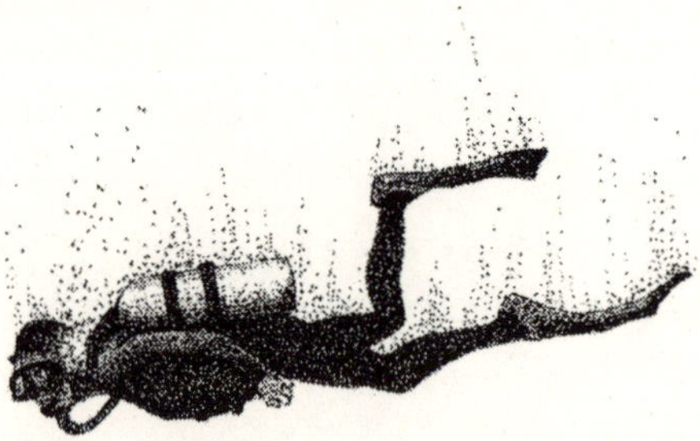

Mail

She found other stuff in the bin, not only the literature left by their case-worker. After dumping her mum's latest cache of pills, she sorted through the streaks of bacon and broken eggshells, bits of old toast and margarine…

Underneath, there were letters, streaked with grease and ripped into ticker-tape.

Some of the letters had been burned with cigarettes. Some were covered in scribble. Others had been destroyed so thoroughly the vandalism looked like an act of devotion.

One of the shreds had her name on it. The full name, intact: Lana Jean Deacon.

After checking her mum was still flat out from the booze, Lana sat at the table, quietly gluing together fragments with a Prit-stick. It was like being one of the archaeologists Miss Rogers had described, like trying to make sense of a dead civilisation.

Our trash will survive us, Miss Rogers had told the class. Our trash will tell future generations who we truly were.

Absolute bits

Dear
distance
a long time
no word, no
worries
as your father .
in this place
and worse
e.g. important birthdays
to explain
But
the words useless
If you are angry
if your mother is
the blame all the blame
the incident
when it occurred
factors
reasons
Call me gone
You, though. This is about
Things
as we are treated
But I was saying
You will never know
how much
this prison
noise

smells
pressure
and the visits
No-one. NO-ONE!
please
If you have it in you
Believe me
Despite my
I
you
to bits
absolute
bits

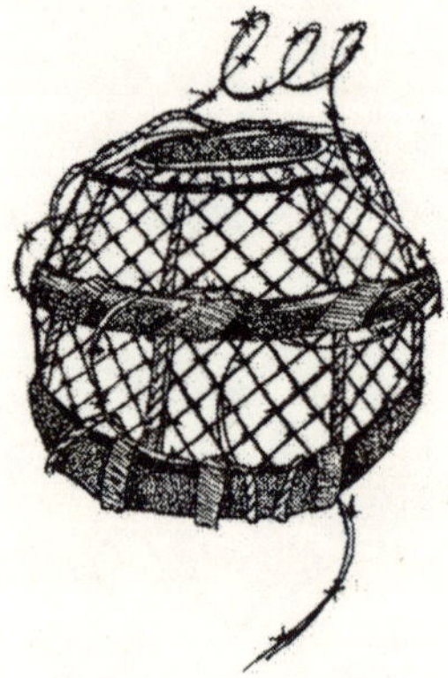

A mistake

After a week of swirling drizzle, the air above the resort turned still. In fierce winter sunshine, the tidal pools shone like church windows.

'Like a summer's day!' said the beach-walkers, as they passed.

But the old man declared the sky too blue. 'Make the most of it, lass; there's summat ugly brewing up.'

As usual, he was clearing the beach of debris, putting items into his sack.

Lana let Ringo force its snout into her face. She giggled, caught up in the animal's joy. People were daft and gloomy. They kept secrets, told lies. They talked about storms when the sun was shining. They hung weights off themselves. Sometimes they hung weights off other people, too.

Dogs were better. You knew where you were with a dog.

'It's got its tongue in my ear, Dad!'

The word was out before she could stop it. It emerged like a solid thing, like a stone.

Mr Flook was either too kind or too deaf to react.

Lana pushed the dog off her, wiped its spit off her ear.

When she was far enough away, she stood alone in the wind. She opened her mouth, let the sunshine in. Afterwards she drubbed her ear with grains of sand, until the last slobber had gone. It felt better then, to be clean. To be calm.

He was way too old, for starters. A man that old, he couldn't even be your grandad, let alone your dad.

'Stupid,' she said. 'You're stupid, Lana.'

Whatever it was inside her that she was blaming, it agreed. 'Yes, you are,' it said. 'You're stupid, Lana.'

Puzzle

He was drawn to a puzzle of fields on the edge of the bay. Those fields were as green as the lawns in a posh garden and had been broken into jigsaw pieces by the sea. You got around by jumping from one green fragment to another. It was like an intelligence test.

Archie spent whole afternoons hopping between the little islands, and passed every test. This proved his theory about school. What use were Venn diagrams? Or that other stuff – statistics and probability? Out here, there were no verbs to conjugate, no bells going off. No-one made you sit in detention, writing lines.

You never had to write anything down at all. Most of the lessons were taught by tides and mud. Often rain delivered classes, too. The longest and most tedious lessons were entrusted to the drizzle. Those could last weeks.

Gasping for breath, he looked back over his latest conquest. He wouldn't get any grades for solving these puzzles made of turf. There were no stars or merits. He'd either survive or he wouldn't. That's what the bay would talk about on parents' evening when it read out his report.

Embarrassment

English people died of it.

They stayed away from the doctor's, and sickened. They stayed away from their friends and withered, alone. That illness, that slip of the tongue – all those embarrassments that made them writhe inside their own skin – it killed them. They died of it.

An embarrassment is patient, though. It bides its time. Often you've forgotten about it completely. Say, you've gone into the streets with your mum, to encourage her. To re-build her confidence. Say, you've seen a shop full of artists' stuff, and you're staring in at the coloured pens and lovely paper. The easels, the pots of ink.

You may even be whistling.

Then, for absolutely no reason, with no trigger, you remember the word that fell out of your mouth. The fool you made of yourself.

Each embarrassment has a different effect on its host. Some people throw up their hands and gasp when the embarrassment strikes. Others wiggle their fingers and make twittering sounds. There are those who push out their lips, say shoo or shush or whoosh.

Lana's embarrassment turned her body stiff. She clenched her arms and grinded her teeth. The noise she made was: 'G-n-n-n-n.'

Mortified, she looked back down the street at her mum, staggering from doorway to doorway. They were doo-lally, the pair of them. They ought to lock them both up.

Foxed

He liked their smell best of all. Often he opened the books just to put his face inside them. It must have been the ink, or maybe the glue in the bindings. The scent of the paper, too. Especially if the book had been kept in a warm window and gone a bit yellow with sunshine.

Not that there were many warm windows, not in a rotten month like February.

Shivering, he pushed the book into his pocket. There had been a lad at his old school, they called him The Brain of Britain. He'd bunked classes because he hated how slow the lessons were. That lad, when they tracked him down, they found him reading in the town library.

Archie wasn't a brain of Britain, not by a long chalk. Numb as a plank, his dad had called him. He'd never been in a library in his life. He liked a good book, though – especially if it had a ship or a boat in it. Or a shark or a reef.

He wasn't interested in discussing the books or learning what they meant. He didn't care if he forgot the story five minutes after finishing it.

Books had the same effect on him as the creeks. They made his head quiet. Often he hummed while reading. That was another reason to steer clear of school. Tucked into a groove in one of the headlands, out of the wind, you could hum as loud as you liked while you were reading.

There was no-one there to call you names, no-one to say you were as numb as a plank.

Garage

When Lana spotted the old man shouldering his sack through the back streets, she was shocked. Until now, she'd only ever seen him on the beach. It was like seeing your teacher outside school. Suddenly you'd no choice but to consider that person a fellow being. He might have a cat and a family. He might go for walks and eat lasagnes.

It must have been the shame made her follow Mr Flook. Maybe she could talk to him, explain about the word that had fallen out of her mouth. She trailed him to a bungalow that backed onto a council football pitch. The pitch was bobbly and rutted with puddles, but the old man's lawn was green and smooth. He showed no sign he knew Lana was there. Instead, he shouted a greeting to someone in the bungalow and went straight to his double-garage, a large flat shed with a shiny red shutter.

Lana had expected the garage to contain one of those ancient timbered vehicles that old blokes fussed over – a Tudor car. But, instead, it was filled by an enormous table, the size of five or six snooker tables. She hovered at the door, watching Mr Flook patiently unload his sack. Tuneless and low, he was singing an odd ditty about a dead horse:

'We'll use the hair of his tail to sew our sail
And the iron of his shoe to make deck nails.'

The table held an intricate map, made of beachcombings. Rivers had been fashioned from lengths of blue netting, headlands lovingly mosaiced from pebbles. The map hadn't been made to scale – here and there, dolls loomed like giants over buildings – but all the finds had been conscientiously restored and set into their exact positions. Dutiful lines marked the sea-depths and lines of latitude.

Lana's eyes roved over the bay, and came to a halt on an ancient fuse-box, carefully painted black, then turned onto its side so that each of its switches formed a window. It was The Property, that horrible building where she lived now.

When the old man answered a woman's summons from the house and disappeared through a door at the back, she couldn't stop herself. Hypnotised, she stepped over the threshold, into the garage.

From fusebox to creel

It stood on the edge of a vast sea which had been jig-sawed together from broken tiles, painted blue and given a varnished gleam.

Lana ran her fingers over the building where she lived, wincing as her fingers met the coarse fuse-wires that the old man had coaxed out from inside, and left poking from The Property. When her fingers arrived at the precise switch where she lived, she found a tiny head looking back at her. The faceless head must have once belonged to a miniature plastic figure, maybe some free gift from a cereal packet that had somehow washed out to sea and been decapitated.

Lana studied the window of her home, dizzy with longing. Was that her mother staring back at her? Or Lana, herself?

Voices, again. Mr Flook talking to the woman who had called him. The sound of a door opening.

Lana lingered by the map. Tiny pieces of sea-glass – green, white, blue – had been shaped into an intricate stained-glass window, part of the ancient church she'd visited on a nearby headland. Everywhere she looked, there were features she recognised. A wrecked big dipper. The stumps of a decayed theatre. As best as Lana could tell, these miniatures had been made from tiny pieces of the derelict buildings. It must have taken him years. He must have been a young man when he began it.

That door again. Muffled voices from the bungalow…

Her eyes were drawn to the bay's far shore, where a fishing creel had been carefully restored, then criss-crossed with barbed wire. Inside, four sombre-clad Action Men, one headless, the others lacking arms and legs, had been tied together with a bike chain. Attached to the creel was one word, set there like a warning. It was a word Lana often found when she went through the torn-up mail in their bin. The name of a prison.

Her gaze drifted from fuse box to creel, across a mosaic of blue tiles. The creel was that close, nearly close enough to touch…

As the door at the back of the garage opened, she lifted her mobile phone to her eye and took a single picture.

She'd turned and gone before the old man shuffled in his slippers into the garage. She was already halfway down the drive.

Storm

It turned ugly, just as the old man predicted. Rain thrashed against the windows. Normally the sea was as thick and slow as gravy, but now white waves were racing in over the flats.

Lana's mum lay in bed, pulling the duvet over her head. She asked if they ought to lay towels on the window-sills.

'*These* towels?' said Lana.

They still didn't know whether the thin grey cloths provided by the landlord were flannels or towels. One of them just about covered Lana's face. If you bunched two of them in your hand, there was some vague chance of getting dry.

Lana's mum pulled the covers tighter. 'The state of those things,' she said. She'd hung the sodden grey cloths over the room's only radiator, which came on in the middle of the night, making them sweat in their sleep.

Her voice muffled, she listed the terrible storms she'd known in her life. Once, she'd stayed up all night, ready for the windows to break. She pitied the trees, having to endure it. Dozens would fall, she was sure. 'You see it on the News,' she said. 'Folk crushed in their cars. Not to mention the black-outs after they bring down power-lines.'

If there was one thing worse than a storm, it was a black-out. No lights at all, everything plunged into darkness.

Lana sat in the window, repeating her mum's words. Plunged into darkness. Plunged into darkness. The phrase made a taste in her mouth. Thrilled, she watched another explosion of rain hit the window. Glass shook in its frame, blobs of water riddled the edgings.

Maybe the storm would blow so hard, it knocked down The Property. Maybe they'd have to move, find a place with better towels. A place with room enough for Lana to bring home friends. A place with the friends to bring home.

In the bag (storm damage)

The crank off an old machine, maybe a mangle.
Needles.
Syringes.
Another Action Man with no head.
One car battery.
Many plastic bottles, many bags.
Half of one porpoise.
The remains of several cuttlefish.
Toddler's sandal (one, red), with damaged buckle.

Stories to tell strangers

My dad? Like I said, off working on an oil-rig.

In the North Sea, yes.

Who said he was probably coming home in the helicopter? *Me*? When am I supposed to have told you that, then?

Last week?

Last week, yes. Last week, that was the plan. To come home in the helicopter, like I told you, if you'd listened properly.

But everything changed after the storm.

You must have heard it on the news, surely.

The accident. When they crashed into the sea and they thought he'd drowned.

I'm surprised you never heard. Maybe you watch the wrong programmes.

Anyway, that was my dad. The only survivor, after the storm.

In the end, he washed ashore, barely alive.

Visit him? In hospital? Yes, definitely. We wouldn't be much of a family if we never saw each other, would we?

But it's a long way to Aberdeen, and he won't even know we're there.

Oh, I thought I'd told you about him being knocked unconscious.

A coma, yes.

After he was battered by the rollers.

So we'll keep our base here for a while yet. Aye, in this boarding house.

Just until we get straight again, and Dad wakens from his coma.

The wave

The sea frightened Lana in the dark. In the dark, its waves moved like skin, as if the water was alive. Often she awoke with the wave coming straight at her.

Tonight, after the dream, she lay sweating under the nylon bedcover, aware of her mother in the bed across the room. There was a trace of drink off her, what Lana's mum called her sleep-medicine.

The room felt very small, with its clutter of brown furniture and murky rugs. The early light picked out bruises on the walls, traces of the people who'd come and gone before them.

Lana stared hard at a spindly mug-tree on the edge of the kitchen sink. Lana hated the mug-tree, and hated being able to see the washing-up from her bed. She threw off the crackly cover and padded across the buckled linoleum to the window. Outside, a baker's van drifted by along the prom. Somewhere far out in the darkness of the bay, a green light was blinking.

There was no gigantic wave, only a brown wash of sea-water, retreating now as the tide fell.

Above, the sky was as grey as a dishcloth. With no stars, Lana used the blinking of the green light, far out across the bay. She matched its flashes to her breath until the dream faded and her head cleared, and she made her wish again, the same wish she made every night after the nightmare woke her.

The hole

After the storm: a hole. Fathoms of blue sky, endless and empty.

The mornings were so glaring, Lana felt as if she was constantly stumbling from a cinema into broad daylight. Away from the sea-front, puddles developed brittle coatings, delicate as toffee apples. When you tapped them, they splintered into fascinating patterns, each delta of cracks a miniature version of the bay.

As for the bay itself, that was too salty for frost, but its pools and creeks went through changes, too. Rather than lying around in their own filth, they roused themselves finally. Lana was dazzled when she splashed through the channels. She felt the light everywhere: on her skin, in her throat. There was sky in the ground, sunlight streaming from the gillimers.

It was so bright, she never saw the walker.

'Aye, it's blinding, alright,' the old woman exclaimed, after the sun-struck girl had collided with her. 'I never saw you either, lass!'

To think – that she could be so clumsy! One person in all those acres, half a mile out over the sands, and Lana bashed into her…

'Well, it takes two to tango,' said the old woman. Unfussed, she steadied herself against her assailant, then began slowly turning. Round, they span, through that glittering ballroom, each of their turns a little faster. It didn't last long, only a few seconds, then they pulled away, giggling shyly, until the old woman curtsied, and they laughed again at their own daftness. Sheila, she said she was called, the old woman – and it had been a while since she last went waltzing. Strange to recall her dancing days, she said. All those years. All the things that happened in a life.

She fell silent. Whatever she'd fixed her gaze on, it was lost in the glare. 'Do you know what they used to call it, this time of year, lass? February?' she asked, at length. 'The season of bright sorrow. Aye, that was their name for it, back in the mists. Don't you think there's something in that? On a day like this?'

Lana nodded slowly. 'I'm sorry for bumping into you. My dad calls me clumsy…'

The old woman straightened her dress. 'Aye, well. Tell your dad there are different accidents, good as well as bad. Say you met someone who knew what she talking about. Someone who's experienced a very bad accident. And this was a good one. So you tell him, girl.'

'Yes,' said Lana. 'Yes, I'll tell him.'

She went on through the shining puddles, thinking about the years, thinking about all the things that happened in a life.

School

Miss Rogers wanted to know if she had anyone to talk to, so Lana told her the truth, for once. 'My mum,' she said.

'And what do you talk to her about?'

Lana shrugged. 'Storms, and that.'

Miss Rogers tried a new tack. What about joining the afterschool club, meeting some new friends? Did she want to learn basketball? Or a musical instrument? The afterschool club was extremely lively, and....

'It can be difficult,' Miss Rogers conceded. 'Difficult to adapt to a new school, especially halfway through the year. Tell me, though: what do you *like* doing, Lana?'

Fortunately the other students were filing in now. Lana wasted time, pretending to rack her brain. Finally, she said, 'I like the beach, miss. I like the sea.'

Miss Rogers nodded. 'Then you're in the right place, lass.'

Lana considered that while Miss Rogers went to the front and prepared her class. It was a startling notion. She resisted the urge to close her eyes as Miss Rogers began the lesson.

There were people who said that evolution meant the survival of the strongest, but the teacher called this hogwash. Evolution wasn't about bullies or violence or fighting. It was about who could adapt. She looked directly into Lana's eyes as she said this. She described a tiny deer on the edge of an ocean, a tiny deer that started to go further into the ocean to find food. Or maybe the deer was trying to prevent itself from becoming food for bigger land animals. Scientists weren't exactly sure why the little deer went into the ocean. But they agreed that it did. And they'd found the bones which proved that the deer one day never returned to the land. They'd found the bones which proved that the deer stayed in the sea and eventually evolved into a blue whale, the biggest creature that ever lived. Bigger than a diplodocus. Bigger than a T-Rex.

'Because it learned to adapt,' said Miss Rogers, holding Lana's gaze. 'Because it survived the pain of its change.'

The law of large numbers

It was probably Archie who'd started it. The mouth on him, he'd probably come out with a threat or a boast. His clothes made it worse, probably: the mud on his shoes, the streaks of dirt over his face. Probably that's why they surrounded him, why they called him Winklepicker, why they called him Peasant.

Probably he was scared of the lads who'd encircled him. Probably he kicked the easiest target. He was a coward, probably. Probably that was why he legged it after he stuck the boot in.

Probably, though, Lana should never have said it in the first place. Probably it all welled up on her. Probably Archie kicked her after it welled up on him, too.

Probably Miss Rogers was right, that you ought to talk about things. Probably, then Lana would never have joined in when she found the others taunting him outside school.

The law of large numbers states that your predictions become more accurate as you gather more data. So let's imagine Lana finds that circle of kids 1,000 times. How many times will she walk away? How many times will she try to break it up? How many times will she join in, shouting, 'Pezz! Pezz!'

To work out the probability, you'd need to live for ages. You'd need to run trial after trial.

Unless you were scared of the answer. Then you probably wouldn't bother.

Duvet

While she was half-asleep and waiting for her mum to finish in the shower, Lana used what her dad had dubbed her superpower: staring into space.

Staring into space, Lana disappeared into the objects in their little room.

Their little room was full of things you never saw until you stared at them.

Until you stared at them, you never thought about interesting things like the curtains.

Interesting things like the curtains contained vast, complicated mountain ranges that tumbled, as detailed as the Andes, from the rail to the ledge.

From the rail to the ledge, Lana let her vision drift, until it came to rest eventually on the duvet her mother had left crumpled on the bed.

Left crumpled on the bed, the duvet had twisted round like a sleeping creature.

A sleeping creature, it lay coiled there, its tail meeting its mouth, the mouth set inside a perfect lion's face, one eye pointing in Lana's direction.

Pointing in Lana's direction, the eye was watching her, she was sure.

She was sure, too, that she must stay where she was, frozen.

Frozen, Lana listened to the shower, still trickling away in the bathroom.

In the bathroom, she would lock the door and save them from the lion on her mother's bed.

The lion on her mother's bed looked back at Lana, only pretending to sleep.

Only pretending to sleep, the lion went on waiting while the shower continued to pour and Lana stared back into its devious eye, whispering: Go away, lion. You're not real. You're only a duvet.

Only a duvet, the lion nodded. And look how frightened you are, girl.

The stone graves

He wasn't stupid. He knew what they called him. Archie's dad had warned him often enough. He ought to shut his geggie, stop talking mince. Waghorn, he'd dubbed his son. Prince of the Liars.

The mouth on him, though. Sometimes Archie vowed to keep it shut. For one whole day, he'd stop bumping his gums.

Then – typical. You tried to get through, but there was someone on the stairs. Someone outside the school. You couldn't get past them. They just stood there, like slot-machines in the arcade.

So you fed them, they were that gormless. You gave them what they were waiting for.

Then afterwards that feeling again, the feeling you got whenever you went down the stairs now. A feeling mixed up with the fust and the mildew. A feeling you couldn't separate from the squidgy red wallpaper that felt like it had once been alive, as soft as a pelt. Touch that stuff, it ruined your day…

So you went far off, into that blank space beyond the boarding house. You walked so far out, you seemed to be searching for the edge of yourself. It was quiet there, following the tide. You heard your actual thoughts.

Then Archie would come back towards the shore again, come back to himself. And he knew they'd be there, waiting to be fed again like slot-machines. The girl downstairs. Her crumbling mother. All the others in that nasty place.

So he stayed out, went down the coast. Climbed the rocks to a headland, where he found ancient graves carved into the sandstone, facing out over the sea. The graves were part of a ruined monastery. Whoever had lain there, they were long gone. The slots were empty.

Archie climbed down into one of the graves. Lying on his back, he watched the clouds go over. A good thought, nearly. One day he'd be as dead as a monk, and there'd be no-one to remember all the mince he'd talked.

The green light

In the middle of the night, Lana's mum found her staring again through a crack in the curtain.

'What is it, love? Another of those nasty dreams?'

Lana shrugged. 'I was watching the flashing light,' she said. 'I think it's a boat… a fishing boat…'

Lana's mother did her famous shiver. 'Back to bed, pet. You'll catch your death…'

They climbed together into her mum's bed. It felt good to lie there like that, warm under the same duvet. Lana slid close and lay listening to her mother's heart, still busily recovering from the day's punishments. She hated the stale drink on her mother's breath, but it was better than the smell of her own sheets, which always seemed to carry some distant whiff of a wet dog.

By the first light of dawn, still awake, she studied the grey threads in her mum's hair, a few more of them now than the last time she'd checked. Most of the hairs came out easily enough with the tweezers, and her mother never stirred.

'Mum,' whispered Lana, winding a hair round her finger. 'Mum – you've got to get yourself together. You've got to look after me, Mum.'

She rolled up the leg of her pyjamas and stared at the bruise left by Archie's kick. It was turning a nasty green colour. Gradually she squeezed tighter, until the pain put little sparks in the dark places behind her eyes.

She could think straight then. She could see everything clearly.

Viking giant

Archie spotted the stone as he trotted home at last, past the open door of the church. It was a hogsback, the sign said – a curved grey oblong that the Vikings had cut to resemble a wild boar. It had lain exposed for centuries in the graveyard on the headland before being dragged indoors. There was another plaque explaining something about the stone's purpose, probably to guard an important grave, but Archie was entranced by the object, and never had time to absorb the words.

He used one finger to trace a stag and a wolf. There were trees too, and what felt to his finger like birds, but it was the snake that held him, a braiding of stone that formed the frame for the carvings. Its scales made the hogsback scary and reptilian, as if a fossilised crocodile had washed up.

What Archie liked most of all was the giant human figure which had braced itself beneath the serpent and raised both arms as if in celebration of a goal. The figure's outstretched arms looked like they were supporting the full weight of the snake. Archie smiled. The figure was going to hoy that massive creature into the sea.

'Can I help you, young lad?'

No, Archie never had the time. He loved an old church until someone in a collar or a uniform turned up, the vicar or the sexton. Then that was that for Archie – he was offski.

He was fast, true. He ran like a hare. What he missed was some muscle. Maybe if he trained, he'd end up like that Viking giant, lift his enemies in the air and throw them in the sea.

Glacier

Falling asleep finally, Archie sat upright in bed, convinced of a truth that was already slipping like sand through his fingers.

Sand through his fingers. Not the sand you saw in films, not fine and white. The brown sludge that sat deep on the bay. Sludge dropped by a glacier, as it died.

As it died, the glacier had unloaded its pockets. That was what he trudged across each day: the small change thrown down by a river of ice, the change it had filched like a thief from the hill country.

Like a thief from the hill country, he ventured there, too – into that strange territory, which no-one was sure whether to call land or water. A place that was both, and neither.

Both, and neither. A boy, a bay.

A bay, a boy. Plus, the tides that crossed them, and made them strange.

The stranger

It wasn't only the stink of booze. The place looked like a double decker had been through it – there were clothes everywhere: a skirt on the carpet, a bra hoiked over the kettle...

How come Lana was back so quickly, her mother wanted to know? What time was it? Had she slept right through?

'Slept right through what?'

Her mum shrugged in that exaggerated way known only to drunks and people making fun of the French. She was sitting in the window with her dressing gown bundled around her. Her head was in her hands, her hands were trembling.

Lana started picking up clothes, then stopped dead. In their bathroom, the toilet flushed. She was holding an unfamiliar pair of jeans.

A shape appeared in the bathroom door, fighting to get a sweater over its head.

'*Dad*?' said Lana.

The shape came out of the bathroom and took the jeans off her. It was a man nothing like her dad. Her dad was built like a heron, long and thin, but this was stumpy puffin of a fella, thick at the waist. He was close enough for Lana to smell the wine off him. There was another smell too, a smell Lana had sometimes caught on the skin of her parents, back before everything went to shit.

'Here,' he said in a blunt little voice – 'your flat is dropping in bits.' And he handed Lana their toilet-chain. 'I'll call you,' he said, glancing towards Lana's mum.

Her mum didn't respond. She sat stock-still while the man wriggled into his jeans and went to the door. It wouldn't open, of course. The lino had bulged. He had to fumble with the handle.

Bang. The door shuddered on its hinges after he forced it shut. And then there were just the two of them again. Or one-and-a-half, anyway. The state Lana's mum was in, she barely counted as a whole number. 'I'm… I'm having the youth your father never allowed me,' she said, pulling the gown tighter.

Lana stood there, holding the toilet-chain.

'Don't look at me like that,' said her mother. 'Grow up, girl.'

Sentence

Yawning and rubbing her eyes, Lana stumbled towards the shower, worried as usual that she'd breathe in spores from the bathroom's fetid air, worried that the spider may have been forced by some obstacle to hang even closer than usual to the mirror where she brushed her hair and that it would get tangled up with the brush and wriggle into her ear, as a kid at school had claimed was possible, not that you could trust the squirts in her class, most of them as bad as Archie, the stuff they came out with: wild boasts and bare-faced lies – for instance, loads more mad stories spouted by the lad who'd invented that nonsense about spiders wriggling into your brain, the same lad who'd claimed that no piece of chewing gum was ever digested by your body, so that all the chewing gum you ever swallowed would still be in your stomach when you died, and if the morticians cut you open with a knife, they'd find it all rolled up together, an entire history of your horrible habits compressed into a solid pink boulder, like the gum they'd discovered inside the life prisoner after he'd snuffed it in his cell of scurvy or something like that, what with the lack of vitamins in him, on account of scoffing junk like chewing gum for twenty years, which, of course, Lana should know all about, her being the daughter of a bloke who was serving a life sentence for…

'Breathe,' she ordered herself. 'Breathe, Lana.' She gripped the sink, held the bathroom steady. It was her own fault for telling people the truth. For being honest when they asked questions.

Calm again, she searched the bathroom for the spider. It was gone: a sign. If the spider could pass beyond the limit of its web, then Lana could too.

The leap

Cockles lived in dangerous places between the tides, gathering in their multitudes on crumbly black outcrops. These were the cockle-cities where they spent their lives, lying in inch-deep holes, filtering sea-water for the plankton that kept them living. Why they were so keen to go on living, the boy had no idea. It seemed a paltry existence, down there in the muck.

Archie had learned to find cockles by searching the sands for what he called eyes. The eyes were two tiny indents, made by the cockle's pipes. There wasn't much more to a cockle than its two pipes, one for sucking in food, the other for expelling waste.

Or so the boy had thought, anyway – until he watched a cockle jump.

It happened in a glittering pool. When the boy peered in, he had a strange feeling of vertigo, as if watching from the sky. A starfish was creeping through the pool, heading towards a cockle. Although he came from far inland, Archie knew what to expect. Maybe he'd watched it on TV, maybe he'd learned it on the streets, but the starfish would swallow the unsuspecting blob of slime that lived inside the shell.

If he hadn't seen it with his own eyes, Archie would have slyly scratched his chin when someone told the story. He'd have called them a liar.

But it happened. A slimy leg sprang out from inside the shell, and the cockle jumped, landing a few inches clear of the famished starfish, which now seemed an awkward, lumbering tank, by comparison. As for the cockle, it packed away its secret leg and slowly returned to the grave where it lived.

Archie watched it sink, until its last traces were those two eyes in the sand.

The eyes seemed to be watching him, just as he'd watched the pool. It made him uneasy. Everything was watching everything else.

In the bag

Toothbrush.
Comb (Mum's, borrowed).
Mobile.
Books for today's lessons.
Letter from Dad (fragments).
List of prison rules (recovered from bin).

Powers

Warily, he scanned the horizon, hearing a faint roar that he sometimes mistook for sounds generated inside his body. The tide was on the turn. Soon this hump of gravel would be flooded. Soon the pool's secret world would vanish.

It ran in the family, his mum said. At home, she'd keep pacing to the window. 'I can feel it on my skin,' she'd say, checking the street again: 'there's a visitor coming.'

Archie had thought it a load of rubbish, his mother's Second Sight. But he wasn't surprised when he saw the girl tip-toeing across the mud towards him. He'd felt her approach on his skin.

He knew things other people didn't. He'd found a pool no other person on Earth would ever see, and watched the famished starfish that lived there. He knew now what lived inside a cockle-shell. Even something so tiny – the strength it contained. How far it could leap.

There were secrets inside everything. There were powers no-one could guess at.

He stayed where he was, hidden under the mound of the cockle bed, humming a song of betrayal he'd learned from his dad:

The Minstrel-Boy to the war is gone,
In the ranks of death you'll find him;
His father's sword he has girded on,
And his wild harp slung behind him.

Soldier

Archie claimed to have been expecting to meet her out on the sand. Second Sight, he said his mother called it. He'd felt it on his skin.

Lana wished he hadn't mentioned mothers.

'Where are *you* off to?' he asked, in his strange way, equally cocky and freaked-out.

'I thought you'd know,' she said, pressing a finger to her temple.

'I never said I read minds.'

'Only predict the future.'

The boy shrugged. He looked as nasty as ever, spit quivering in the corner of his mouth, narrow shoes scumbered with mud. 'I'll predict one thing,' he said, casually – 'if you keep heading that way, in three days from now, they'll find your body.'

'It takes an expert, does it?'

'If you like. But I never called myself an expert.'

'What, then?'

'A soldier,' he said. 'I call myself a soldier.'

Lana let out a laugh. 'That's why you go round kicking girls, is it?'

'One girl,' he said. 'I only ever kicked one girl, and she was a coward. She was only brave in a gang.'

Lana resisted the urge to soothe the injury he'd dealt her. A cold wind ruffled the puddles. Her skirt was thin, her legs bare. 'Seeing as you asked, I'm off to the other side,' she said, at length. 'To see if I can put things right with my dad.'

The boy lowered his eyes when she mentioned her dad. Lana spotted that. All the guff he talked about frogmen and soldiers. That was when she guessed.

'Get a bus,' he said, sullenly. 'Take the train.'

'What with, washers? I'm skint. Besides, someone will notice. They'll be looking.'

'An important person, are you, eh?'

She heard the bitterness. 'No,' she said. 'No, I'm not important, except to my mum.'

'And your *dad*,' he said, keeping the tone of resentment.

'My dad? My dad only likes me when I'm not there.'

Archie seemed to chew on that for a while. He turned away without speaking. But when he glanced back from further down the channel, she understood she was supposed to follow him.

The tower

'How the hell were you hoping to get there?' he asked, leading Lana into a narrow creek.

'By aiming for the green light. The green light on the other side, like in *Gatsby*.'

'That isn't on the other side. It's in the middle of the bay. You were heading for the light on the sewerage tower.'

Lana frowned. 'You know everything, don't you?'

'I know where the shit comes out,' he said.

A joke

She liked him better when he was busy. He was quieter, he didn't boast. His coarse white fingers worked adroitly on the knots that held the boat to its mooring.

Without speaking, he slid the boat over the mud, into the reeds, then nudged it out into the peaty channel that gurgled around Lana's feet.

'Whose is it?' she asked.

The boy shrugged. 'Ours,' he said. 'For a bit, anyway. Until we return it.'

She climbed in, ignoring the hand he offered. It was bad enough needing his help; she didn't want to touch him, too. 'Are you sure you know where you're going?'

'I know this place like the back of my hand,' he said.

Suddenly he screamed so loud, Lana almost toppled out of the boat. He was holding the back of his face to one eye and shouting in a deranged voice, 'What the hell's *that*? What the hell *is* it?'

A joke, he said later, when the boat was still again. Couldn't she take a joke?

No, she told him. No, a joke was supposed to be funny.

Then how come it wasn't funny when she'd joked around, he wanted to know? Outside school?

Lana stared ahead, soothing the bruise on her shin. When, finally, he dug the boat's only oar into the creek's calm water, she took a breath again.

The boat

It leaked, of course. Lana's job was to bail out water with a silver jug, evidently tarnished from years of the same work.

Plus, its name.

'Who the hell calls a boat Ian?' she asked.

Archie went on rowing. 'Why not?'

'Boats are women,' she said. 'Everyone knows that.'

'Maybe it's not the boat's name, maybe it's the owner's. Or the owner's lover. Maybe the owner's gay.'

Lana shook her head, still bailing with the jug. 'You can't call a boat Ian,' she insisted.

Archie said it didn't matter what the boat was called. It mattered only that she kept bailing. Could he rely on her to perform that one simple task?

'If you avoid wrecking us on a skear,' she said.

'It's bad luck to say things like that,' he warned. 'Haven't you the sense you were born with?'

'No,' she said. 'Otherwise, I wouldn't have climbed into this sieve, would I?'

'Keep bailing,' he said. 'Keep bailing and shut your mouth.'

The change

He'd headed in the usual direction, floating down to where the creek met the river. Then he pointed the boat into the flood. There, the river bumped up against the returning tide. It was a moment he always liked, when he'd to straighten the boat. A struggle to put muscles on your arms. A struggle fit for a giant.

But, today, he knew his arms were no match for it.

A river has a mind of its own. It kinks around to avoid one obstacle and charges directly at another. There are shallows and depths, not always in places you expect. Also, slack spots and rapids.

He guessed what had happened. During the storm, the river had found a new channel. His normal route had been closed. They were heading in the wrong direction.

'Keep bailing,' he ordered the girl, digging into the water as she shouted something back at him. 'Keep bailing and don't talk!'

Flood

They floated out to meet the returning flood, with no control over where they were heading. She was trying to show him her phone. 'Look!' she said.

'Now?' he said, incredulous.

The boat rucked beneath them.

'The map,' she was shouting. 'On the 'phone! The old man's map.'

Water was entering the boat.

'Bail,' he told her. '*Bail!*' He dug deeper with the oar. The boat span like a coin. If they were lucky, the incoming tide would sweep them back to shore. If they weren't, the river would carry them in whatever new direction it had devised, maybe miles out to sea.

She was still sticking the phone in his face. When he pushed it away, she lost her grip and it fell in the river. Then she was slapping him, shouting. Meanwhile all he could do was stare at his hand, still smarting from where she'd slapped it.

'The oar!' he cried. 'The oar's gone!'

The tree

As far as he could work out, they'd been pulled at least a mile downriver before the boat began to sink. But now, already, they'd somehow made it back to shore. Thrilled to feel solid ground under his feet, Archie let out a trembling whoop.

Then, as Lana pushed him up the beach, he realised his error. They hadn't found the shore, only a sandbank, far out in the bay. He wiped his eyes and tried to focus, still coughing up sea-water. Already, even as they staggered over the mud, the incoming tide was flooding the bank. In a few minutes, it would be gone.

'There!' said Lana, pointing. She pulled him over the bank's smooth curve and plunged them into a flood of grey water on the other side. Then they were shambling through a freezing channel, up to their waists in swirling water. 'Keep going,' she urged. 'Straight ahead.'

Archie's breath came in shivering gulps. The rushing water was tugging and pushing him, reaching his chest now, threatening to rise to his face.

'The tree,' she cried. 'Straight on, for the tree.'

It was a hawthorn, stunted and bent sideways by years of wind and rain. Somehow it had taken root there on that speck of rock in the sea. Dripping wet and freezing cold, they knelt before it in wonder.

Orders

As soon as they crawled ashore, Lana knew what to do. After settling the coughing boy beneath the hawthorn tree, she marched into the brushy undergrowth that covered the tiny island and began snapping off long, dry blades of grass and weed.

She returned to find Archie trembling so violently she was afraid he'd break his own teeth. But it was all clear to her, and she never wavered. She scooped sand from the bank where Archie was lying, and lined the pit with grass.

'Here,' she pointed. 'Out of the wind.'

The soldier followed his orders. He lay down beside her and watched her piling undergrowth over the hole. There, they passed the next few hours, trading what little warmth remained to them, under a rough covering of weeds.

She never told anyone, but it was her mum's TV programmes that saved them. Without those stupid documentaries, the boy would have shivered himself into a fit.

Lantern

At first, she thought the green light had somehow loosed itself from its moorings and drifted out of the darkness, to find them.

Then she heard his voice travelling over the water:

> '*We'll use the hair of his tail to sew our sail*
> *And the iron of his shoe to make deck nails.*'

As he turned the corner of the island, she saw the lantern on the back of his boat, and knew for sure the old man would save them.

The habits of whelks

It was only later he confessed the truth about his dad. He wasn't a frogman who swum down to the sea-floor to untangle cables. Drink had got the better of him after he was discharged from the army. Then he ran up gambling debts and left home. Later – no-one had told Archie exactly when – he killed himself. His wino mates found him hanging from a rafter in the derelict house where he'd shacked up.

Maybe it would have been better if Archie had told her this while they were shivering together through that long night on the island. Maybe it would have brought them closer.

As it was, Archie moved on soon afterwards, and Lana never saw him again. She remembered him, though, and hoped he sometimes remembered her.

He'd been a pain in the neck, true. He'd called himself a soldier and kicked her leg. There was always a bit of white spit hanging off his mouth and he'd had those horrible eyes, bonfire-red. The skin on him too, all pale and crusty.

You didn't meet many people like him, though. He went wherever he wanted. He covered the bay.

No, they hadn't grown an inch closer while waiting for rescue, even though they clung to each other for warmth. She didn't tell him about her dad and he never spoke about his. All through the night, until they saw the lantern on the old man's boat, he'd kept Lana awake, telling her about the habits of whelks.

For years afterwards, she thought twice before joining a crowd, though, and never again entered a small boat. So he stayed part of her, whether he knew it or not, as strangers sometimes do.

She hoped he'd found someone to listen when he went on for hours about whelks. He was what Lana called a character.

Dear Dad

I hope you are keeping well, as we are here. Thank you for your letters. I have found it interesting to piece together your life in the prison. It sounds hard, especially the pressure. Living near the beach, I've got used to the peace and quiet.

I'm sorry for not seeing you yet. When I tried to visit, I had to come home again, because of some circumstances. Don't worry, though – Mum is feeling a fair bit better, and says we'll do our best to put things right. First, we need to flit again, though. The Property where we live has been condemned, and the council are looking into some options. We'll be glad to move from what we call Hell House. Even the spiders don't like it here.

But I hope we can stay by the sea. I've made some new friends and I like the beach, so you don't need to worry. There is an old man who has a dog called Ringo and a boat with a lantern, and I go out for walks with his wife, Sheila. She gives us jam, for the vitamins. When she was young, she liked to go dancing. The town was lively, then.

It isn't anymore. But the quiet is better. In your letters, you mentioned the noises in prison, and I wished I could put the sound of the sea into this envelope for you. I think it would do your soul some good. That's a saying I learned from the old man. He comes out with stuff like that, from the olden days. He says he hears the cockles singing. He talks about The Living Waters. Recently I went out in his boat with him and one of the new friends I mentioned (see above).

It was cold in the boat with the old man and my friend. We saw a light flashing in the distance, and I imagined it was the light on the prison. Maybe you could feel me thinking about you? There are people like that, I've heard. People who get prickles on their skin.

When we were out in the middle of the bay, where it was really dark – almost pitch-black – the old man told me I had a choice in life: to either focus on the lantern or focus on the night. To shine my light or cast my shadow.

I wanted to write that here because it's been on my mind. But I have to go now, because it's time for school. If I don't see you through the week, I'll see you through the window (joke!).

In haste, with love,

Your daughter, L

The Map

He'd guessed the river was up to its old tricks, and had been keeping his spy-glass trained on the bay. Live as long as him, you felt it on your skin.

They were waiting for their mothers in the old man's bungalow. His wife Sheila fussed around them, telling Lana not to bother about the mud they'd brought in.

'Do you two know each other?' Mr Flook asked them.

'We sometimes go dancing together, eh, lass?'

Privately, Lana nodded at the old woman and took another pull on the hot milk. At her side, Archie worked deeper into his blanket, silent after their long vigil in the hole.

She was feeling better now, Lana announced. Before their relatives came, could she maybe do one thing? Have a gander at the map that people had told her about?

Mr Flook smiled, knowingly. 'Word's got around, has it?'

'Amongst the chosen few,' she said.

The old man came after her into the garage. His dog brushed against her legs as she rounded the enormous table and retraced her voyage.

'I was heading here,' she said, pointing to the creel.

'Aye,' said the old man. 'Aye, I'd worked that out, I think, lass.'

South from the creel, and then a few miles west along the coast, she found a tiny cross, the place she guessed where the couple had suffered their loss.

He had his reasons, of course. The constant beachcombing, the endless task of the map. People go to strange lengths to preserve a memory.

Lana wondered whether it was a son or a daughter. One day soon, she'd come back and thank them. She'd bring the old woman flowers, and introduce them to her mother. It would be good for her to mingle instead of sitting alone in the window, shivering.

'Cold, lass?' Mr Flook asked.

'Just a bit,' she said.

Together, they went back along the map, into the bungalow.

About the Author

David Swann started out reporting on Accrington Stanley's football matches for the local rag. Later, working in Amsterdam, he became a toilet cleaner at the legendary Paradiso nightclub. He now teaches at the University of Chichester. His short stories and poems have been widely published, including nine successes in the Bridport Prize and two in the National Poetry Competition. Some of his very short stories were gathered in 'Stronger Faster Shorter' (Flash: The International Short-Short Story Press, 2015). Dave's collection, 'The Privilege of Rain' (Waterloo Press, 2010) – based on experiences working as a writer-in-residence in a jail – was shortlisted for The Ted Hughes Award.

About the Illustrator

Sam Hubbard is an illustrator, designer and contemporary artist from West Sussex, where he lives by the sea with his wife, two young daughters and Persian cat. When away from his drawing board he works as a Creative Director of a design agency and can usually be found running, swimming, or drifting around in his little boat on the river Arun. More of his work can be found on Instagram @5am.illustration

Acknowledgments

David Swann would like to thank the following for blessing this little boat: Jude Higgins and John at Ad Hoc Fiction, and Michelle Elvy, the 2021 judge. I count myself a lucky man to have sailed for years with Ed Hogan; Bethan Roberts; and Karen Stevens. Ahoy there, me hearties! For charting the sands, and parts thereabouts, I thank Linda Anderson; Pete Barnes and family; Alan Burns; David Craig; Martin Elvins; Ian Marchant; and Saleel Nurbhai. I acknowledge support from students and colleagues at The University of Chichester. The following people have often dug me out of the mud: Geoff, Jennie, Steven and Joanne Swann; Rachel Hughes; Vaughan Wilkinson; Piet, Truus, Ellen, Karin, Mirjam, and Angela Vermond; Jan Willem Sligting; plus the many very lovely Rowleys, Sligtings, Verbeeks, Hallenslebens, Hugheses etc. For giving this old wreck a harbour, thank you to Peter Blair and Ashley Chantler. 'I look deep down and do believe' thanks to several past shipmates: Tonya Blowers; Simon Finch; William Gray; Josie Harbutt; Steve Haywood; Simon Jenner; Chris Jones; Jemma Kennedy; Mimi Khalvati; Stefano Luzzatto; Ton Marar; Stephen Mollett; Jago Morrison; Stephanie Norgate; John O'Donoghue; Natalia de la Ossa; Michael Raine; Henry Shukman; Huw Taylor; and Tim Ward. A special cannon-blast for recent crewmates: Charlotte Brunsdon; Jonathan Carr; Greg Challis; Ele Cogo; Peter Davison; Hugh Dunkerley; James Ebdon; Naomi Foyle; Norie Fujimori; David Gilliver; David Hesmondhalgh; Mathilde Heu; Jeannette Laouadi;

Michael Loveday; Anke Mittelberg; Lucy Morris; Janet Paske; Ernesto Priego; Roger Rees; Helen Steward; Tim Vickery; Linda Webb; and Stewart Wills. And, finally, to the calmest skipper on the waters, Sam Hubbard – shiver me timbers, we did it, Sam! 'The world's a ship on its passage out.'

SAM HUBBARD would like to thank the following: Miriam Hubbard, Lynda Hubbard, Mark and Natasha Debnam, Anne O'Brien, Amy and Paul Halls, the Gisbey family, and of course, Captain of the ship (and lockdown pen pal) David Swann.

Praise for *Season of Bright Sorrow*

'*Season of Bright Sorrow* is a little miracle. David Swann takes a boarding house, a boy, and a bay; a girl and her mum; a scattering of glimpses and gaps; and he gives you nothing less than the universe. There's warmth and wisdom, here. Heartbreak, profundity, and humour. And beautiful drawings, too, by Sam Hubbard. It's a short book, and it's absolutely full to the brim with love.'
~ Edward Hogan, author of *The Electric* (John Murray, 2020).

'*Season of Bright Sorrow* is by turns dark and foreboding, life affirming and hopeful. Each flash fiction is unique and haunting, and together they reveal our human urge for connection and certainty. Swann's characters possess you instantly and we cannot help but enter fully into each strange and beautiful life.'
~ Karen Stevens, author of *Writing a First Novel* (Palgrave, 2014).

'In a series of poetically precise and illuminating flashes, this novella explores how one girl, Lana, begins to learn how to live in a world full of loss. David Swann finds a specific language for a specific landscape, and, in doing so, connects with universal themes of grief and hope. It's beautiful. And it's funny, too.'
~ Bethan Roberts, author of *My Policeman* (Vintage, 2012).

'Dave Swann's portrayal of childhood brims over with wisdom, warmth and wonder. The coastal settings are so achingly desolate, the characterisations so astute, idiosyncratic and compassionate throughout. *Season of Bright Sorrow* feels note-perfect and yet it's full of wildness and wilderness. There is an unforgettable magic at work.'
~ Michael Loveday, author of *Three Men on the Edge* (V Press, 2018).